Helen and the Hudson Hornet

Helen and the Hudson Hornet

by Nancy Hope Wilson

illustrated by Mary O'Keefe Young

Macmillan Books for Young Readers • New York

To my brother Rod,
whose appreciation of junkyard beauty proved contagious
—N. H. W.

To Taylor, whose sweet face moved my brush,
and to my brother Terry, who knows why
—M. O'K. Y.

~~~ ❖ ~~~

Macmillan Books for Young Readers
An imprint of Simon & Schuster Children's Publishing Division
Simon & Schuster Macmillan
1230 Avenue of the Americas
New York, New York 10020

The text of this book is set in 13.5-point Galliard.
The illustrations were done in watercolor.

Printed and bound in Singapore on recycled paper
First edition
10 9 8 7 6 5 4 3 2 1

Library of Congress Cataloging-in-Publication Data
Wilson, Nancy Hope. Helen and the Hudson Hornet / by Nancy Hope Wilson ;
illustrated by Mary O'Keefe Young. — 1st ed.
p.   cm.
Summary: Although five-year-old Helen is upset when the old car stored in her family's shed is sold,
the new owner eventually returns with a special gift for her.
ISBN 0-02-793076-9
[1. Automobiles—Fiction.] I. Young, Mary O'Keefe, ill. II. Title.
PZ7.W69745He 1995
[E]—dc20   93-32321

Helen's favorite smell on earth—better than lilacs in spring, better than popcorn in a movie theater, better even than her mother's pillow—was the inside of that old car in the shed.

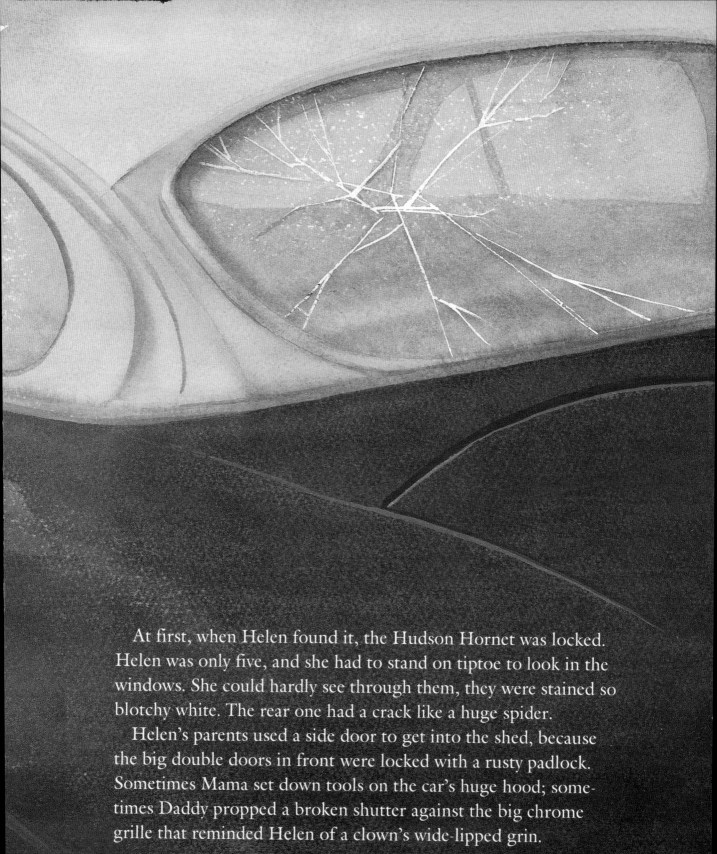

At first, when Helen found it, the Hudson Hornet was locked. Helen was only five, and she had to stand on tiptoe to look in the windows. She could hardly see through them, they were stained so blotchy white. The rear one had a crack like a huge spider.

Helen's parents used a side door to get into the shed, because the big double doors in front were locked with a rusty padlock. Sometimes Mama set down tools on the car's huge hood; sometimes Daddy propped a broken shutter against the big chrome grille that reminded Helen of a clown's wide-lipped grin.

Then one day they came home to the steady honk of a deep, booming horn. Unbelievably, it came from the shed. Helen's parents hunted frantically for the old car key, while the horn commanded the neighbors to stand around watching nothing. The sound was already fading when Mama finally pried the horn loose with a screwdriver, and silence rushed in.

After that, the Hudson Hornet was left unlocked, and Helen could explore it at last. The seats were cracked and torn, but gave off a soft, oily smell that made Helen close her eyes and breathe deeply. Pipe smoke still seemed to cling to the fringed plaid car blanket that lay moth-eaten in the backseat. In the glove compartment, Helen found a pipe, and a map so old it had worn through at every fold, and under those, a pair of real leather gloves. Helen often took out the pipe, the map, the gloves, looked at them carefully, then replaced them exactly as they'd been.

Now Helen drove everywhere in the Hudson Hornet: to the circus, across the ocean, and to her secret land of Windamere, where cars could talk and children made all the rules. The steering wheel grew warm and smooth in her hands. She could only pretend to honk the horn, but she remembered its booming voice, and used it to scatter all enemies.

When she arrived, she climbed into the backseat. Sometimes the blanket was a circus tent, and her world smelled of elephants and hay. Sometimes the blanket was a sail, and her world smelled of oilcloth and salt air. In Windamere, she wore the blanket like a cloak while the Hudson Hornet whispered stories about its old friend the wizard. Then her world smelled of oil and wool and pipe smoke again.

One summer afternoon when she was tented under the blanket,
Helen heard her father's voice outside the big double doors:
"Hope this key works. Never dreamed anybody'd *buy* this car."

Helen threw off the blanket and kneeled to look out the rear
window. Her eyes were just adjusting from the dark of the tent to
the dim light of the shed when the doors flew open. Against the
blinding sunlight she could see only the outline of her father and
another man, their shapes made all crooked from the spider crack
in the glass. Helen slid to the floor. She curled up with her head
on the big bump in the middle, and pulled the blanket over her.
She lay still, but her breath whirled like a storm about her face.

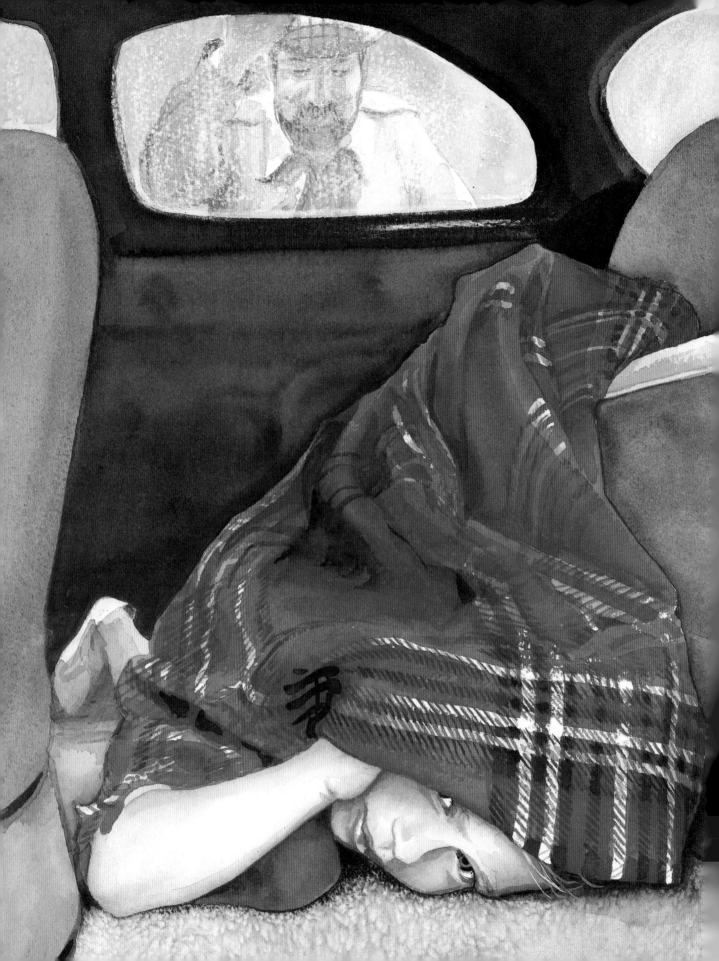

Daddy walked around the car with the stranger, pointing out the crack in the window, the chrome in good condition. Helen heard the car hood pop and creak open, then groan as it was slammed shut. The stranger didn't speak, but Helen could imagine him clearly: beady eyes, fangs. She knew he was drooling, just waiting to pounce like the Big Bad Wolf.

Then suddenly the driver's door opened.

"My daughter loves it in there," Daddy said. "She'll be awfully sad when it goes."

Helen heard the stranger take a deep breath. She waited for his snarling laugh. "I *love* that smell!" he said instead. Helen almost gasped. How could he have such a smiley voice? "I'll have to meet your daughter," he added. "Bet we'd like each other."

But Helen was sure she'd *never* like the man who was taking her Hudson Hornet.

When the truck came a few days later, Helen hid in her bed with the old car blanket over her head. In her lap were the pipe, the map, the gloves. She had yelled with anger and cried till her stomach hurt. Her parents had been understanding and comforting, but the truck still came. She could hear it clanking and grabbing at the helpless car. She would not look out the window. She would not watch the Hudson Hornet dragged into the sunlight.

Fall passed. And winter. Helen stayed away from the shed, but she could feel its hollow emptiness inside her. Now her parents called the stranger their friend, and he came with his wife to the Saturday night card games. Helen refused to meet him, but she

could hear his cheerful voice as she turned over in her sleep. The treasures from the glove compartment had a special place on her bookshelf. If she held them and closed her eyes tight, sometimes she could still smell that favorite smell. But it didn't bring back the Hudson Hornet.

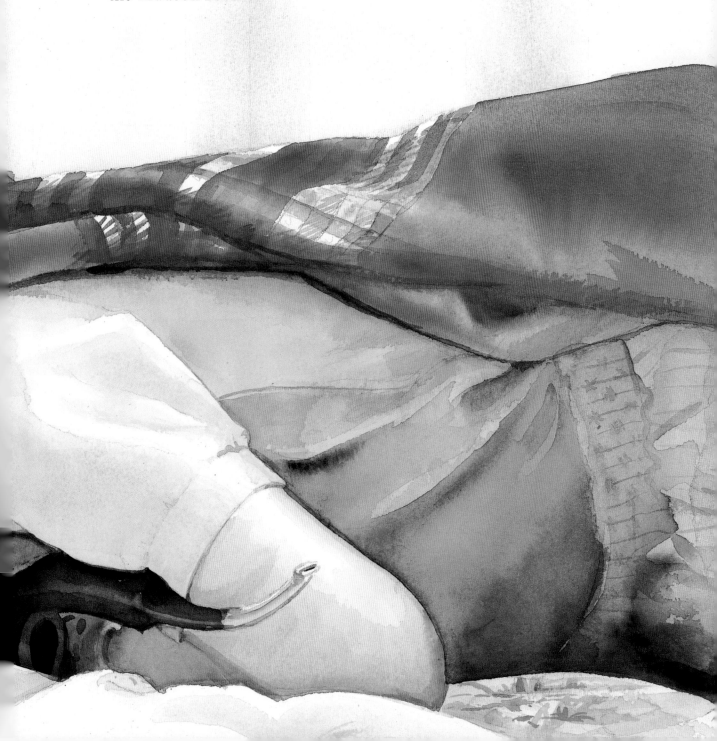

Spring came, and Helen turned six. One drizzly afternoon, she sat propped up in bed with the car blanket and a pile of books. When she heard a deep, booming honk, it fit right into the story of ducklings trying to cross a city street.

Then she heard it again. She threw off the car blanket to run to the window, but she caught herself and turned away.

"Helen!" Daddy called. "Someone's here to see you!"

When Helen reached the kitchen, the stranger extended his hand. "Name's Roger Bliss," his familiar voice said. "Call me Roger. Got a car out there needs your approval."

The hand that shook Helen's didn't feel at all slimy. Helen looked at Roger sort of sideways. He was tall and thin like Daddy, and his friendly eyes seemed to like her already.

"Come on," he urged.

"Go on," Mama coaxed with a smile.

With her raincoat on, Helen stood on the kitchen stoop and stared, amazed. There in the driveway was her Hudson Hornet. Even the gray drizzle couldn't hide the gleam of its creamy new paint job, the smooth shine of the seats through startling clear windows.

Roger opened the passenger door as if for a queen. The seat felt like velvet, and its rich, oily smell filled the car.

"Sorry," Roger said as he climbed in, "I don't smoke a pipe." For the first time, Helen looked straight at him, and felt a smile creep on to her face.

The Hudson Hornet rolled majestically away from Helen's house. She sat up tall in the great throne seat. She could see the whole, deep sky through those clear, clear windows. Roger shifted gears. As the powerful engine churned, the Hudson Hornet seemed to sail through the world like a huge, soaring ship.

They rolled through neighborhoods Helen had never seen. Roger found several excuses to lean on the horn that shone, now, like a moon in the center of the steering wheel. Helen sat silent with her hands in her lap. She felt fizzy, and full to the brim. With each deep, booming honk, she thought she'd overflow.

She unlatched the little triangle window and aimed the wind full on her face.

"Where'll we take her next time?" Roger asked.

Next time? Suddenly Helen bubbled over with laughter. She would still go places in the Hudson Hornet. "Everywhere!" she shouted through her laughter and the wind.

As they turned toward home, Helen noticed the glove compartment and reached to open it. It was empty. She clicked it shut with a sadness she couldn't quite hide from Roger.

"Wish you could've seen my other Hornet," he said cheerfully. "My old Brown Betty. Sold it to keep this one."

"What's this one's name?" Helen asked.

"Just wondering that myself," Roger answered. He gave the horn one last, long honk as they turned into the driveway at home. Helen scrambled to push open her door and climb out of the Hudson Hornet. "Hey!" Roger began.

"Just a minute!" she called back.

Her parents looked like surprised blurs as she ran through the bright kitchen and up the stairs. "What's up?" they asked as she headed outside again, but they could see the answer.

Helen climbed back into the Hudson Hornet and opened the glove compartment. Gently, she laid the gloves in their place, then the map, then the pipe on top.

"They still sort of smell right," she explained.

"Thank you," Roger said solemnly.

Helen smiled. "Got a name yet?"

"Not yet." Roger rested his hands loosely on the steering wheel and stared out toward the old empty shed. Helen sat back in her seat, cocking her head forward a little to watch him think.

"How about Humdinger Helen?" he said at last.

Helen giggled with satisfaction and reached to click the glove compartment shut. She wasn't quite sure what *humdinger* meant, but she knew it must be good.